NOTHING SPECIAL

written by

Desiree Cooper

illustrated by

Bec Sloane

WAYNE STATE UNIVERSITY PRESS • DETROIT

African American Life Series

Melba Joyce Boyd, Editor

Department of Africana Studies,
Wayne State University

A complete listing of the books in these series
can be found online at wsupress.wayne.edu.

ISBN (hardcover): 978-0-8143-4973-1
ISBN (ebook): 978-0-8143-4975-5

Library of Congress Control Number: 2021952555

Cover illustration by Bec Sloane. Cover and interior design by Chelsea Hunter.

Wayne State University Press rests on Waawiyaataanong, also referred to as Detroit,
the ancestral and contemporary homeland of the Three Fires Confederacy.
These sovereign lands were granted by the Ojibwe, Odawa, Potawatomi, and Wyandot nations,
in 1807, through the Treaty of Detroit. Wayne State University Press affirms Indigenous
sovereignty and honors all tribes with a connection to Detroit. With our Native neighbors,
the press works to advance educational equity and promote a better
future for the earth and all people.

Wayne State University Press
Leonard N. Simons Building
4809 Woodward Avenue
Detroit, Michigan 48201–1309

Visit us online at wsupress.wayne.edu

To my parents, Willie and Barbara,
who traveled the world but never left home.
And to Marilyn Nelson, who planted this seed
that magical Sewanee summer. —D. C.

For Hazel & Emmett, and their nana,
Paveena, with all her sunflowers. —B. S.

Jax jumped out of the car and ran into his grandparents' arms. It had taken a whole day to drive from Detroit to Virginia. He thought they would never get there, but they made it!

That night, Jax wondered what he would do with his grandparents during his summer vacation. Maybe they would take him to the zoo, or buy him toys at the mall, or share popcorn at the movies! He fell asleep thinking about the fun day ahead.

"Good morning, Jax!" his grandfather woke him with a kiss. "Good morning, PopPop!" Jax said, leaping out of his bed. "What are we going to do today?"

"I think we'll do some of the things that I did as a boy," PopPop said.
"Like what?" Jax asked.
PopPop smiled and said, "Nothing special."

Jax hopped into his grandfather's red truck. Soon, they were at the beach. Jax looked inside PopPop's bucket. There were hooks and string and lumps of raw chicken.

"The tide is high," PopPop said. "We'll catch lots of crabs." They put chicken on the hooks and sank the strings into the water.

Jax sat beside his grandfather on the pier in the morning sun.

They sat and sat. The water splashed.

The seagulls squawked.

On the end of the string, a big, blue crab grabbed the chicken.
"The line is moving!" Jax jumped up and down.

Jax held the string while PopPop netted the crab.

And another.

And another!

Before long, they had enough blue crabs for dinner.

On the way back to the truck, Jax could hear the crab claws tap-tap-tapping in the bucket. Crabbing was better than going to the zoo. But Jax worried that he wouldn't get to do the things he liked to do in Detroit.

"Can we go to the movies now?"
he asked when they got home.
Instead of answering, PopPop went into
the house and came out with a newspaper,
two sticks, tape, and old string.
"What are you doing?"
Jax asked.

PopPop tied the sticks into a cross. "Help me tape the newspaper to the sticks," he said. When they finished, PopPop held it up. "It's a kite!" Jax exclaimed.

At the park, Jax ran while the kite danced in the sky.
He thought their kite wouldn't fly as high as the other
kites that came from the store. But it did!

Soon, it was time for dinner. Jax hoped PopPop would
take him to the drive-thru to get a hamburger and a toy.
But PopPop said, "Let's go home and help Nana cook."
Jax felt sad that they didn't go to his favorite place to eat.

When they got home, Nana handed them a basket.
"Can you shuck this corn?" she asked.

Together, PopPop and Jax pulled off the green husks. The husks felt like paper.

"What's this stuff?" Jax asked. It was stringy like hair, but very sticky. "It's called corn silk," said PopPop.

When they finished, PopPop laughed.
"You look like a scarecrow!" he said,
brushing the corn silk from Jax's hair.

"This is better than hamburgers, Nana!" Jax said, holding up a crab.
"Thank you, Jax," said Nana, kissing the top of his head.

That night, they sat on the porch swing and watched the fireflies. Jax tried to count them, but he had to keep starting over.

There were so many!

Snuggling between his grandparents, Jax thought about his day. He hadn't gone to the zoo. He hadn't gone to the movies. He hadn't even eaten a hamburger.

Still, it felt like all of his wishes had come true. He went crabbing. He flew a kite that he and his PopPop made. He feasted on crabs and corn, and he got to sit outside and count fireflies.

Jax listened to PopPop hum. Suddenly, a star shot across the sky. "Jax!" PopPop said. "Did you make a wish?"

"Yes, PopPop," Jax said. "I wished for nothing special."

Author's Note

I'm an Air Force brat who was born in Japan in the early 1960s. After traveling the world most of my childhood, I spent my adult years raising a family in Detroit. There, I became a Pulitzer Prize–nominated journalist, an award-winning author, and an activist for women's rights.

Despite living in Michigan for 30 years, "home" always remained the birthplace of both of my parents—a little town in the piney woods of central Virginia. Like so many other black families in the North, we religiously made the pilgrimage back South every summer to attend family reunions, church "homecomings," and to remain connected to our Southern roots. Much is said about the Great Migration when more than six million African Americans left the oppression and violence of the Jim Crow South between 1910 and 1970. But little is said about the annual reverse-migration that has become central to black nostalgia. *Nothing Special* is an homage to that cherished tradition.

After a lifetime away, I've returned South to help my parents through their final years. I live near Virginia Beach in the family home where I'm now welcoming new generations through these steadfast doors.

Desiree Cooper

Illustrator's Note

I've always gravitated toward the old ways, finding kinship in traditions like storytelling and sewing by hand.

Naturally, I found there was just one way to bring *Nothing Special* to life. As a homespun tale of finding connection across generations, it called for that human touch. Through my signature textiles, each with tales of their own, I invite readers to share in that connection.

Over the years, I have employed my craft in film and theatre, children's media, education and animation, reintroducing audiences to the textures and patterns of shared familiarities: Reimagined and thoroughly dissected, an old tote bag gives us thousands of leaves for a magnolia tree. A sock gives us its blossoms. Piece by piece, I gathered the materials to build the elements of Jax's world, each intentionally chosen to play its part. Together, they reveal the evolving narratives among ordinary things. At a certain angle, you might even call them nothing special.

Bec Sloane